First American Edition 2015
Kane Miller, A Division of EDC Publishing

Text, design and illustrations copyright © Lemonfizz Media 2010
First published by Scholastic Australia Pty Limited in 2010
This edition published under license from Scholastic Australia Pty
Limited on behalf of Lemonfizz Media

For information contact:
Kane Miller, A Division of EDC Publishing
P.O. Box 470663
Tulsa, OK 74147-0663
www.kanemiller.com
www.edcpub.com
www.usbornebooksandmore.com

Library of Congress Control Number: 2014949838

Printed and bound in the United States of America
6 7 8 9 10

ISBN: 978-1-61067-382-2

JUMP START

19-21-19-1-14-14-1-8
13-3-6-1-18-12-1-14-5

Kane Miller
A DIVISION OF EDC PUBLISHING

6-15-18   5-13-13-1

9-14-19-16-9-18-1-20-9-15-14

1-14-4

3-15-14-19-21-12-20-1-14-20

23-9-20-8   12-15-22-5

Chapter • 1

The school gym was really buzzing that afternoon. The music was blaring and the girls were laughing, but there was still a lot of hard work being done. Everyone wanted to do their best at the state gymnastics meet, just weeks away.

Emma Jacks really wanted to do her best, but right now she was standing on the beam, stressing.

Emma couldn't do it. She wanted to do it. She thought she really should be able to do it. And everyone else seemed to be doing it, which made things worse—a lot worse. But no matter how hard she tried, Emma could not do the high jumps on the balance beam.

Every time she tried, she seemed to chicken out and do a tiny jump instead. So tiny her coach could hardly see it. And if she couldn't do the high jump, there was no way she would do well in the state meet.

"Come on, Em, you can do it," said Hannah, one of the girls on Emma's team and also one of her best friends. "You jump high all the time when we're just messing around. Just don't think about it so much."

"How can I not think about it, Hannah!" Emma replied. "It's the one part of the routine I never get right and the season is about to start. If I can't get the high jumps right, I'll let the whole team down."

Lauren, who was Emma and Hannah's coach, had been listening to the girls talk.

"Hannah's right, Emma. You just need to believe in yourself a bit more. We all do. Come on, what's the worst thing that can happen?" she asked, and then answered her own question, "You fall off."

"Yes, but then I lose *big* points!" said Emma. Having just missed out on a medal last year, she really wanted one this time, for herself and the team. But that was never going to happen if she fell off—or if she didn't do the jump.

"But if you don't even try the jumps, you won't get any points anyway," said Lauren. "Think about the jump, not the falling off. You know you can do this, but you think yourself out of it. In fact, Em, maybe don't think at all. Just trust yourself and do it."

Don't think. That was hard for Emma. She loved thinking. She thought about things all the time. Even as Hannah and Lauren were talking to her now, she was thinking how her friend's name was spelled exactly the same backward as forward: H-A-N-N-A-H, like E-V-E and R-A-D-A-R and R-A-C-E-C-A-R and her favorite, Y-O B-A-N-A-N-A B-O-Y.

"Emma, are you still with us?" laughed Lauren.

"Oops, sorry," said Emma. "I was just thinking about…"

"Aaaaaaaaaaaaaaaargh," cried Hannah, waving her arms in the air. "Just do the jump!"

"Okay, okay!" said Emma. "Don't think it, just do it."

It was Emma's turn on the beam. She took a deep breath, presented, with her arms stretched up and out, and then started her routine. As always, she talked herself through it.

Jump off the springboard and onto the beam. Do the squat and hold—one, two, three seconds. Keep your legs over the beam. That was hard! Okay, high left kick to the front, high right kick to the front, keep upper body in and present. Not bad! High left kick to the back, both hands up in the air, put the left leg back…

Emma was halfway through and so far, so good. She spun around at the end of the beam.

Okay, it's jump time. Big split jump to the right, big split jump to the left. Don't think about it. Do it!

But just as she was thinking about not thinking, Emma felt her muscles tighten and her mouth go dry. She could feel herself starting to panic.

Don't panic. Just do what you can and finish the routine. Stay on the beam, don't fall off, stay on the beam!

She did the first split jump to the right—not a big one, but she was still on the beam. Then she did the split jump to the left, which was even smaller than the first one, but at least she had stayed on the beam.

Almost done! Handstand, pretty good I think, now turn on both feet and run to the end of the beam. Dismount and stick the landing. Present with a big smile!

It was over. It wasn't great, but it was over.

"Nice jump," smirked Nema. "That was a jump, wasn't it?"

Nema was one of the girls on Emma's gymnastics team, but she was definitely *not* one of Emma's best friends—at least, not anymore. The two girls used to be friendly, but now Nema seemed more interested in her hair, which she flicked a lot, and being randomly mean to people. Emma didn't bother answering.

"Hmmm, good kicks and great dismount," said Lauren. "But where were the jumps? I know you can do it, Emma. Just go for it. Next time I want to see really *big* jumps, even if you fall off the beam. In fact, I want you to fall off!"

Emma groaned. She knew she couldn't avoid the jumps next time. Lauren would make sure of it.

Now it was Nema's turn. She presented with a flourish, flew onto the beam and completed the routine without a single mistake. She even threw in a new trick from the next level.

"Perfect, Nema!" Lauren clapped.

Nema turned and beamed at Lauren. "Thanks, coach," she said, and then with a sideways look to Emma added, "I really love jumping!"

"I really love jumping," Emma repeated quietly, in a high-pitched voice. A perfect routine from little Miss Perfect, she thought. *Little Miss Mean Perfect!* But then it was Hannah's turn and her attention turned back to her friend.

Hannah almost skipped through her routine. She did two fabulous split jumps but then fell off the beam as she balanced for the handstand. As quick as a flash, Hannah got back on, did a brilliant handstand, ran down the beam and ended with a perfect dismount.

"Good work, Hannah," said Lauren. "Just settle yourself after the jumps before going on to the handstand."

"No probs," said Hannah, cheerfully.

Why didn't Hannah mind about falling off? Why didn't Hannah mind about anything? And why didn't Nema have anything to mind about?

It would be Emma's turn again soon. There was only one thing she could think of that would get her out of doing her routine again—a mission alert for EJ12!

Chapter •2

Emma was an average ten-year-old girl. She went to school, which she liked, most of the time. She had a family that she liked, most of the time—but not always all at the same time. Life went on pretty much as normal—sometimes really good, sometimes a little bad, sometimes a bit nothing.

Emma's favorite color was blue—aqua, actually. Emma liked to be exact about these things and there were some awful shades of blue around. She also liked purple and orange, but not together. She liked apples, pears, mandarins and grapes, but she did not like bananas or grapefruit. She did like banana milkshakes though, but thought that banana and chocolate milkshakes were much, much better. Emma liked chocolate. Correction: she *loved* it. Correction: she *adored* it. In fact, there was not much Emma would not do for chocolate. Luckily she also loved swimming, basketball and gymnastics!

When she was not eating chocolate or playing sports, Emma loved emailing her friends, irritating her brother, drawing and reading about animals. Actually, Emma loved animals even more than she loved chocolate.

She also liked math. Emma didn't care that some people thought it was a bit nerdy. She just liked the way you could count on math. She liked the way the numbers made up patterns and how you could usually tell what was coming next. But most of all, Emma liked numbers because they made sense, they didn't give you mean surprises, and you could rely on them.

Doing math was relaxing for Emma. It wasn't that she didn't find it hard sometimes because she did, it was just that she liked sorting out the problem, she liked making things make sense. One plus one was two. It was *always* two—it didn't just sometimes decide to be three or maybe four and then say, "Only joking, two really." Five times five had to be twenty-five, not 467 or 34,589! It would be twenty-five tomorrow and the next day and all the days to infinity. It didn't matter what you were wearing or whether you invited it to a sleepover or not, it would always be twenty-five. Emma wished that some of the girls at school could be that reliable.

It was actually math that started it all—"all" being the one thing that was not so average about ten-year-old Emma Jacks. Emma was a secret agent. She was EJ12, a field agent and code-cracker in the under-twelve division of **SHINE**, a secret agency that protected the world from evildoers.

Emma was selected to join **SHINE** when she won an elementary school math contest. **SHINE** needed clever thinkers, especially people who loved math, and didn't seem to mind if they were still in elementary school. **SHINE** needed agents to help them crack the codes and thwart the missions of evil agencies like *SHADOW*. **SHINE** tried to defeat *SHADOW* by intercepting their secret messages and foiling their dastardly plans.

In some ways, Emma would have been just as happy simply cracking the enemy codes and letting some other field agent go on the missions, but that was not how it worked. **SHINE** had a motto (quite a lot of mottoes actually), "If you crack the code, you take the load." So Emma, or EJ12, or just EJ, as she was called when she was on duty, would be sent on missions all over the world.

When she was EJ12, Emma seemed to be able to do incredible things. She could scale high walls, fly hang gliders and skate across glaciers. She remained calm under pressure and always seemed to know what to do in a crisis. In fact, she seemed to be able to do things that would completely freak Emma Jacks out—why was that? Was it the special equipment **SHINE** supplied? Emma wasn't sure, but she often wished EJ12 could sometimes go to school instead of her and she wished EJ12 could be the one to do gymnastics meets!

Emma pulled her mobile phone out of her gym bag. She flipped open the screen, hoping for a message. Nothing. It was a very cool phone though, a cross between a game console and a phone, with lots of applications. Many of the apps were top secret, hiding behind the normal ones on the screen. When **SHINE** wanted Emma for a mission, her phone would vibrate and the screen would flash aqua. (You could select your own alert color and Emma had, of course, chosen her favorite.) But right now the phone wasn't doing anything. It was most definitely, unfortunately, doing nothing at all.

Well, at least she had a mobile phone now, even

if it wasn't flashing. At first, Emma's parents had been firmly against letting her have one.

"You don't really need a mobile, do you, Em?" her mom had said. "Why can't you just use the home phone?"

Use the home phone? Really, was she serious? Emma loved her mom, but she did wonder about her parents sometimes. Why did they think that mobile phones were just for calling people? What about music, photos, text messages, apps and joining the twenty-first century.

Piinngg!

Suddenly there it was—saved by the flash! (A nice aqua flash.) Mission alert! *Excellent*, thought Emma. *No more no-jumps today!*

"Sorry, Lauren, I've got to leave early," said Emma, grinning at Hannah as she headed toward the door.

"But you'll miss your next turn on the beam," said Lauren.

"Oh, what a pity, but sorry, can't help it, got

to go," called Emma, as she grabbed her bag and rushed out of the gym.

Not for the first time a mission alert from **SHINE** had saved Emma's day!

Chapter • 3

Emma ran to girls' bathroom, quickly checked that no one was there and turned on the hand dryers. The noise of the hand dryers would be important in hiding the noise of what was going to happen next.

Emma did often wonder why she had to report in to **SHINE** in the girls' bathroom. It was not really what she had imagined during her secret-agent training. She was sure there were more secret, spy-like and glamorous ways to start a mission than sitting on a toilet—but perhaps that was the point. Who would ever suspect that a top secret international mission was getting underway in the girls' bathroom?

Emma went to the last stall on the right. With one more quick glance around the bathroom she closed and locked the door. She dropped her gym bag, put down the toilet seat, sat down and flipped open the toilet paper holder. If you didn't know what you were looking for, you would never notice a small electronic socket on the side of the holder. Emma pushed her mobile phone into the socket and waited. There was a beep, then Emma entered her pin code and removed her phone. Another beep and then a message flashed up on her phone screen.

WELCOME BACK EJI2
HOLD ON!

EJ picked up her gym bag, grabbed the edge of the toilet seat and counted to three. On three, the wall behind the toilet spun around, with the toilet and EJ still attached. EJ slipped off the toilet seat and onto a waiting beanbag. A protective shield lowered itself down and clicked into place over the beanbag. She was at the top of a giant tunnel slide. It was the **SHINE** Mission Tube. EJ typed "go" into her phone…

WHOOOOOOOOOOSH

EJ loved this bit. For the next two minutes she had the best giant slide ride of her life as she whizzed around the corners and down the straights of the **SHINE** underground tube network.

The tube was the secret transportation system of the **SHINE** agency. It carried its agents from their home tube to different **SHINE** locations, including **SHINE HQ** where agents were briefed for their missions.

She finally came to a halt at a small platform with a keypad. The shield flipped back. She keyed in her pin code and waited for the security check. This changed every time she started a mission. Sometimes it was fingerprints, sometimes an eye scan, sometimes hair samples. You never knew what it would be—and neither would anyone trying to break into the **SHINE** network.

"Please sing the first line of the Australian national anthem," requested a digital voice. *Great*, thought EJ. *Voice recognition.* She didn't mind singing in the shower, but that was about it. She cleared her throat and sang.

"Australians all, let us rejoice!"

"Louder, please," requested the digital voice. *Thank goodness no one is listening*, thought Emma, feeling her cheeks blush. She took a deep breath then belted out the line again.

"Australians all, let us rejoice!"

"Slightly out of tune, but agent identity confirmed. Please drop in, EJ12!"

There was a beep and the floor seemed to fall away as EJ dropped down into a small chamber. The beanbag was perfect for a soft landing.

EJ was now in the Code Room, a small chamber with nothing in it except a table, a chair and a clear plastic tube coming from the ceiling directly above her. There was a whizzing sound and suddenly a small capsule popped out of the tube and onto EJ's lap. It was the first code.

Whenever **SHINE** intercepted an enemy message, they dispatched it to one of their agents for decoding —the faster the better. That was another reason why **SHINE** had the underground tube network— it got the code to the agent quickly. **SHINE** could connect their network to the best location for each agent, which in EJ's case was the school bathroom. Hmmm, perhaps she could convince them to have a second location.

In the Code Room, EJ opened the capsule and took out a small piece of paper and a pen. She always felt a bit nervous opening the enemy message. Would she be able to crack the code? What if she couldn't? She unfolded the paper—there was nothing there! EJ turned the paper over. The other side was blank too!

It was unlike **SHINE** to make a mistake so there had to be something she wasn't getting. EJ thought hard. *If I can't see the message it must be invisible*, she thought. *Invisible…invisible ink?* It was worth a try. She searched through the top secret apps on her mobile phone and then touched one of them on the screen. A small but strong purple light came on—violet actually. EJ scanned the paper with the light and as she did, the message appeared.

She read carefully.

EJ laughed out loud. "They're going to have work harder than that," she said to herself. "This will take no time at all!" She opened up another app on her phone screen and scrolled down. She knew exactly what she was looking for.

Gotcha!

A	B	C	D	E	F	G	H
1	2	3	4	5	6	7	8
I	J	K	L	M	N	O	P
9	10	11	12	13	14	15	16
Q	R	S	T	U	V	W	X
17	18	19	20	21	22	23	24
Y	Z						
25	26						

Within minutes, EJ had broken the first two lines of the code.

16-18-15-2-12-5-13   23-9-20-8
P R O B L E M W I T H
16-18-15-10-5-3-20   7-18-5-5-14   5-25-5.
P R O J E C T G R E E N E Y E.

The next bit was trickier. *Why suddenly have letters in a number code? That doesn't make sense.*

Or does it? EJ had an idea. *If there are letters where there are numbers, there are probably numbers where there are letters. Let's see if this works…*

EJ remembered the maps they used in class. *If I'm not mistaken*, she thought, *that's a map reference: 2S 68W!*

The last bit was easy. EJ had now cracked the whole code and she wrote the message underneath.

For EJ12's Eyes Only

(Message intercepted from SHADOW)

16-18-15-2-12-5-13   23-9-20-8
P R O B L E M W I T H
10-18-15-10-5-3-20   7-18-5-5-14   5-25-5.
P R O J E C T   G R E E N   E Y E.
18-5-16-15-18-20   2-21-20-20-5-18-6-12-25
R E P O R T   B U T T E R F L Y
20-18-5-5   B19   FH23   6-15-18
T R E E 2S 68W   F O R
9-14-19-20-18-21-3-20-9-15-14-19.
I N S T R U C T I O N S.

But what did it all mean? What was Project Green Eye? What was the problem and what on earth was the Butterfly Tree? EJ folded the paper, put it back in the capsule and lifted the capsule back up into the mouth of the clear plastic tube.

WHOOSH!

The capsule was sucked up and away, rushing toward **SHINE HQ**. Which is exactly where EJ was heading next.

Chapter •4

The decoded message would beat EJ to **SHINE HQ**. This allowed the **SHINE** support team enough time to work out what she would need for the mission. By the time EJ whizzed into **SHINE HQ** there was already a backpack and field agent gear laid out on the briefing table. And in front of the table stood an older lady in a smart black suit and a beautiful yellow pendant necklace. It was A1, the head of the **SHINE** agency.

"Good morning, EJ. Good to have you back— nice ride?"

"Fabulous as always, thank you, A1," EJ replied.

EJ really liked A1. She was the one who prepared agents for their missions, and also the one to go to when things got tricky. While that explained the 1 in her code name, no one seemed to know what the A stood for. Her first name perhaps. Amy? Alice? Alexandra? EJ didn't think A1 looked like any of those names. In fact, she reminded EJ a lot of her grandmother. A1 had lovely pure-white hair swept back into a bun, which she often used to hold pens and pencils—and once a flashlight—she was using. EJ knew better than to be fooled by the white hair though—it was the *only* old thing about A1, who ran three miles every morning and was still the agency's record holder for long-distance swimming.

A1 seemed to have been at **SHINE** forever. EJ wondered how long. She wondered lots of things about A1, but never seemed to find any answers. EJ had also heard other agents talk about A1 having a sister. There was an agent, code name A2, who worked for **SHINE**, but one day she vanished with some secret plans **SHINE** was working on and was never seen again. Did she go across and start working for *SHADOW*? Was she really A1's sister? Some agents believed so, but there was never any proof and no one was brave enough to ask A1 what happened.

"Daydreaming, EJ12? Anyway, good work on the first message," A1 congratulated her. "You were right. It was a simple number-letter match and by cracking it so fast, we can get this mission off to a quick start. Now let's see what we know already." A1 stepped back. "Light Screen lower," she said loudly.

An enormous plasma screen came down in front of them. EJ loved the Light Screen. It was voice-activated and powered by **SHINE**'s giant computer system. It could show information from anywhere on the Internet, as well as **SHINE**'s own secret files, all within seconds.

"Show message," said A1, and the message EJ had decoded in the Code Room flashed up on the screen.

```
PROBLEM WITH
PROJECT GREEN EYE.
REPORT BUTTERFLY
TREE
2S 68W FOR
INSTRUCTIONS
```

"You were right about the map reference," A1 explained. "Earth Map." A map of the world appeared on the large screen. "Find 2 South, 68 West," A1 directed, and within seconds the Light Screen had zoomed in on what looked like a huge blob of green.

"But there's nothing there," said EJ.

"Wait a little longer," replied A1.

And sure enough, as the map focused and came into view more clearly, EJ could see that the green was made up of trees—hundreds and thousands of trees.

"More detail, show images," instructed A1.

Images began to appear on the screen: an enormous river surrounded by deep-green rain forest, then pictures of monkeys, birds, butterflies, enormous and beautiful flowers. It was a tropical paradise.

"Amazing!" EJ sighed.

"It is now," said A1, "but not for much longer, I fear. This is the location that corresponds to the coordinates in the code, so it must be pretty close to Project Green Eye—and whatever that is, you can bet it's not good. We have been gathering information on *SHADOW's* recent activities. The information suggests that *SHADOW* has been preparing to build a new satellite dish in a remote area that no one has ever been to. With an extra dish in a new location, *SHADOW* will be able to get more information to their agents—and quicker too. Their ability to send and receive communications will be second to none—not to mention their surveillance capability. If this new satellite dish becomes operational, we might not be able to intercept their messages. Who knows what evil plans they will make?"

"And, if they're planning to build it at *this* location, it won't be any good for the rain forest," added EJ.

"Exactly, EJ12," said A1. "So we have two reasons to move extremely quickly."

Suddenly a red light started to flash on the Light Screen.

"Oh dear," said A1. "Make that *three* reasons. The red light indicates that *SHADOW* has discovered that we have intercepted their message. They won't want to take any chances, so they'll assume—correctly—that the message has been decoded. That means they know we're on to Project Green Eye, so we'll have to move quickly."

SHADOW messages usually worked in a particular way. When they needed one of their agents to do something, *SHADOW* would send a message, but the message would be in a secret code and they would use several messages to deliver the full set of instructions. There could be two, three, even four messages for the complete set of instructions.

SHINE was always on the lookout for these messages from *SHADOW* and they looked for suspicious emails, letters and texts. They needed to get the message before the *SHADOW* agent did. If they did manage to intercept a message, they then needed to decode it—and that's where agents like EJ12 came in. Once an agent had cracked a code, it would often direct them to another message and then to another. But they had to work quickly to stay one step ahead of *SHADOW*. If *SHADOW* realized that a message had been intercepted, they might be able to destroy the other messages before the SHINE agent got to them or they might send a *SHADOW* team after the SHINE agent. Neither of those things was good. There was one more catch. *SHADOW* was always trying to find ways to stop SHINE being able to get their messages or inventing new ways to send them that SHINE would not detect. Sometimes the *SHADOW* codes would change and get harder with each message so an agent had to keep on her toes.

And now it looked as if *SHADOW* knew **SHINE** had their message. EJ12 would have to move fast—and carefully.

Chapter · 5

"Okay," said A1. "We'd better jump to it. We know where to send you…"

"Yes, but what is the Butterfly Tree?" EJ wondered aloud.

"That we *don't* know, but finding that tree is the only way to intercept the next message from *SHADOW*. Unfortunately we won't be able to drop you right at the location," explained A1. "The forest is too thick and we may be detected. We can get you pretty close, but then it's up to you. Your mission kit is ready, so let's get you started."

EJ looked over the gear on the briefing table: standard **SHINE** cargo pants, backpack, **SHINE** belt, boots and T-shirt, compass, flashlight, binoculars, insect-repellent spray and sunscreen.

EJ smiled when she saw the boots. They looked like your standard-issue mission boots, but they could convert into practically anything: skis, stilts, ice skates or even jumping springs. EJ wondered if they had been upgraded. While the boots were very clever, the various bits of equipment did seem to come out rather randomly which could cause problems. However, EJ didn't want to seem rude so she kept quiet. Then she spied a pair of sunglasses.

"I bet they do something pretty clever," said EJ enthusiastically. She couldn't wait to hear what clever invention the **SHINE** scientists had added to these quite ordinary-looking glasses.

"They protect your eyes from the sun," said A1, looking slightly surprised. "What else did you think they might do?"

"Oh, I don't know," said EJ, feeling slightly

embarrassed. "X-ray vision, perhaps? Infrared night vision goggles?"

"You've seen too many spy movies, EJ12," laughed A1. "Gadgets can be fun, but sometimes the best tool an agent can have is her own common sense. Remember the motto: 'An agent's best gadget is her brain.'"

EJ nodded and tried to look like she agreed. She wondered if A1 had kids– that common sense line was classic mom speak. EJ was a bit disappointed.

A1 must have realized because she smiled and said, "And as always, there are a few extra charms for your bracelet."

Yes! thought EJ, *Now we are talking!* Out of all the mission gear, the charms were her favorite. **SHINE** invented the CHARM equipment system for agents to be able to carry gear easily and without being detected. Named for Clever Hidden Accessories with Release Mechanism, the system was made of gear and gadgets shrunk into small silver charms that were then worn on a bracelet on the agent's wrist. The gadget was released and restored to normal size when the agent twisted the charm. *Incredibly handy—and, rather cool,* thought EJ.

An agent would receive new charms for each mission but could also keep charms from previous missions that might come in handy. EJ always kept her skeleton key charm on but didn't always carry her baby penguin food!

A1 produced a small velvet bag containing the charms for the mission: a butterfly, a crocodile, a heart with wings and a key.

"But I already have a skeleton key," said EJ.

"We know, but it's time for an upgrade," replied A1. "Your other one was getting a bit old and being up-to-date is key for SHINE agents!" she said, chuckling at her own joke. "There's no time to go through the rest now but remember to twist the charms to activate them."

EJ looked at the charms more closely, especially the crocodile. She really *really* hoped she would not need that one.

"Okay, EJ12, we're running short of time," said A1, winding up the meeting. "There will be a further briefing once you are on your way. As soon as you find the second message and crack the code, make contact again. By then, we may have discovered important information about whatever *SHADOW* is up to this time. But for now, jump to it, EJ12, and good luck!"

"Will do," EJ replied. What was it with all the jumping today? She went into the dressing room and changed into her mission gear. Cargo pants, belt, T-shirt, boots, even a hair elastic for a ponytail. **SHINE** always thought of everything and that made EJ feel safe and confident. Finally she slipped the new charms onto her bracelet and she was ready— for anything.

A1's voice came over the loudspeaker in the dressing room. "Agent EJ12, *Shineforce 10* is ready for you now."

"Awesome!" cried EJ, coming out of the dressing room and meeting A1.

Excellent, she thought. *Shineforce 10, the jet— my favorite!*

SHINE had many ways of getting agents around the world quickly and secretly, but super-sleek *Shineforce 10* was definitely one of the best. It had delivered EJ to deserts, tropical islands and snowy mountain ranges and she couldn't wait until she was allowed to fly it herself. She had already earned her mini-wings, which meant she could take control of SHINE choppers and hot air balloons, but the agents in the Under-12 division were not allowed to sit for their mega-wings license, mainly because they were still too short! *Oh well*, thought EJ with longing. But it was still unbelievably cool to be a passenger on *Shineforce 10*. And to think that her dad was still worried about her going home alone on the school bus!

Chapter •6

E J boarded the super-shiny silver jet, and looked around with an enormous smile on her face. This absolutely made up for the girls' bathroom at the start of each mission! There were only four seats on the plane and they were huge—much more like little couches than airplane seats—with lovely deep cushions and a control panel that moved the seat and backrest any way you wanted them. You could even spin the whole chair all the way around!

E J snuggled in and strapped on her seat belt. At the far end of the cabin she could see the pilot,

LP30, in the cockpit, going through her last-minute preflight checks.

"Welcome aboard, E J12. Good to see you again!" she called over her shoulder. "I'll just get this bird up and running, then I'll come back to you once we're at cruising altitude."

EJ loved the takeoff. She loved the rush of speed as the plane thundered down the runway, and then the almost magical way it lifted off the ground and climbed into the clouds. The houses and cars became smaller and smaller and then completely disappeared and the plane seemed to float along on a fluffy bed of cloud. As she looked out the window, EJ's thoughts wandered back to the gymnastic meet and the routine on the balance beam. Twisting her bracelet around in her fingers, EJ went through her entire beam routine in her mind, from start to finish. Well, almost. But even when she did the routine in her head, she still stopped when it came to the high jumps. All she could see was Emma Jacks falling off the beam. Why was that? Why couldn't she do an amazing split jump instead? What was stopping her?

EJ knew the answer. She was stopping *herself*—but how on earth did you stop yourself from stopping yourself?

Suddenly the intercom interrupted her thoughts.

"EJ12, we are now at 30,000 feet and it's time for your in-flight briefing," said LP30. "Please turn your phone to in-flight mode and watch the screen in front you."

A small screen popped out of the wall in front of EJ's seat, and there was A1.

"Hello again, EJ12. I hope you are sitting comfortably. Please listen carefully to this mission briefing. As you know, you are flying to one of the world's most remote rain forests. You know a lot about animals, but in case you come across any you don't recognize, you'll be able to learn more about them using your phone. Just take a photo of them and the information will appear. The wildlife in this area is protected—it's a World Heritage site. But be careful, EJ. The rain forest is beautiful and filled with some of the world's most unique animals, but many of them can also be dangerous."

The screen flickered momentarily and then A1 continued.

"Your mission, EJ12, is to find the Butterfly Tree and get the next set of instructions. Once you have done this, please report back to SHINE HQ. EJ, I can't stress how important it is that we find out where Project Green Eye is and shut it down before it can do any damage—to us and the rain forest.

"Whatever *SHADOW* is up to we know it's going to be bad. Endangered animals are at risk as well as beautiful natural rain forest habitats. You are aware of the environmental risks and what it will mean for our planet. Project Green Eye must be stopped!"

A1 paused and reached for a glass of water, then she resumed the briefing.

"Finally, you will also need to activate the BEST system in your phone. Remember, you can only choose one contact, so choose carefully. Good luck, EJ12. **SHINE** out."

SHINE knew that no single agent could know everything that might need to be done on a mission. That's why they had developed the BEST system for agent assistance.

BEST = Brains, Expertise, Support, Tips.

Every agent had a network of "BESTies" who were screened by **SHINE** and authorized to help the agent, if possible, on missions. There were two conditions though: the BESTies could ask no questions and agents could never discuss their work with them outside of their missions. It was much too risky. EJ's BESTies thought it was pretty cool, even if they couldn't talk about it. After all, how many people have a secret agent for a friend?

EJ opened the BEST app on her phone and flicked through the photos of her friends. Who would be best able to help her on this mission? What was she going to need? There was not much to go on, but EJ did know one thing. She would need to stay calm and the best person to help her do that was Hannah. Nothing seemed to get Hannah flustered or upset, which was sometimes a little irritating, but also meant that she was a good friend to have around when EJ started to stress. When Emma was on the beam, she could almost feel her friend's support, as if she was doing the routine with her. Hannah would be perfect for this mission.

Just as EJ was about to press OK to activate Hannah, Hannah's photo started flashing—Hannah was calling her.

"Hey there, how did you know I was OM?" (EJ thought that was better than saying on a mission— you never knew who might be listening. She also thought it sounded like rather good spy speak).

"Oh, OM! Sorry, I just wanted to tell you about the change to the beam routine. It was decided after you left," explained Hannah.

"No!" said EJ. "Please don't say there are more jumps!"

"Okay…" the phone went silent.

"Well, then?" asked EJ.

"You told me not to say…"

"Hannah!" cried EJ.

"You asked me not to say it, but, yes, there are more jumps. Lauren thinks we have a better chance of earning more points that way, and she thinks everyone is doing great jumps," Hannah finished.

"Everyone except me," said Emma, rolling her eyes.

"No, that's not what she said—and, before you say it, it's not what she thought either. No offense, Em, but chill a little! You get so jumpy," Hannah laughed. "Hey, that's quite funny! Anyway, Em, what's the big deal? You're actually a really good jumper when you put your mind to it. Just do the jump and get on with it! What's the worst that can happen?"

"I fall off, lose massive points, get no medal, let the whole team down," said EJ, feeling that this summed up the whole disastrous situation rather well.

"You won't get a medal if you don't jump at all," said Hannah. "Isn't it worse to know that you won't even have a chance of winning if you don't try?"

"Yes, but…" began EJ, when suddenly, the intercom came on again.

"Okay, EJ12, it's time for the jump," said LP30. "Prepare your landing gear."

Gee whizz, lemonfizz—what is it with the jumping? thought EJ. *Well, at least this is one jump I can do! I can jump down—it's up that I have the problem with!*

"Gotta go, Hannah, but I've uploaded you as my BESTie for this mission, so be alert!"

"Of course, Em, we always need more lerts."

"That joke is never funny, Han. See you!"

"Okay," laughed Hannah. "Just don't go overboard, Em. I'll be here for you."

Hmm, not overboard exactly—but out of the plane, thought EJ. She pulled on her parachute, double-checked her straps and gave LP30 the thumbs-up. The hatch door opened and EJ jumped out of the plane and into the blue sky.

Chapter · 7

As she passed the last wisps of cloud, EJ looked down and the ground below became clearer. She was thrilled to see how the enormous river twisted and turned around the rain forest, just like a giant turquoise snake weaving its way through the lush green trees. The closer she came, the better she could see just how dense the rain forest was. **SHINE** had been right. There was no way a plane would have been able to land there. In fact, EJ wasn't sure she could land there either.

And if she couldn't land on the ground, that only left the river. EJ thought back to her briefing—crocodiles, piranhas and water snakes. That didn't make a river landing an attractive thought. She needed to land safely, but how? As the water loomed up toward her, EJ decided that it was definitely time to see what her boots would do this time. She just hoped it would be quick.

EJ clicked her heels together and waited. She watched as the soles of the boots swiveled around and two shiny ice skates appeared.

They were great in Antarctica, thought EJ, *but somehow I don't think they are quite what I need now.*

She clicked again and this time, the ice skates retracted and two coil springs popped out. *I don't think so. Please, third time lucky,* thought EJ. She was nearly down now and would soon hit the water. She clicked again and this time flippers came out. EJ hoped she wasn't going to have to swim. She looked down at the water. Now that it was so close, she could see that the river was wide, very wide, maybe a mile across. Could she swim it with her parachute and her backpack? And even if she could, what else would be swimming with her?

EJ really needed the boots to give her something better. She clicked again and held her breath. This time, there was a whirring sound and two boards shot out from under the boots. *Great*, thought EJ, *water skis—but I assume there's no speedboat in there with them.* "Stupid boots!" she shouted and crashed the skis together. As she did so, the boards clicked together and a pole shot up at the front of them, a handlebar unfolded at the top and a small engine dropped down underneath. *Clever*, thought EJ. *I take it all back.* With only feet to go before she hit the water, EJ was now on a small water scooter. This was going to be fun!

She pulled the rope on her parachute straps and the chute disappeared into her backpack. As she touched the water, she squeezed on the handlebars and she was off, skimming her way along the river. And to think that her dad wouldn't let her ride her bike on the road yet!

EJ switched on her GPS navigation system (another thing her mom didn't realize you could use your phone for) and set it for 2 South 68 West. From the map, she could see the route she would take. She would have to move off this big river into a smaller one, but for now there was quite some way to go. That was just fine with EJ. She could enjoy the view—but not for too long. *SHADOW* wouldn't be far behind and there was no time to lose.

Everywhere EJ looked, there was something new to see. The river was as wide as five freeways and seemed to have a new bird or animal living around every bend. She looked up and there was a flock of brightly colored macaws, rich blue with golden-yellow tummies, screeching above the trees. They settled on some palm trees where they cracked open coconuts with their beaks. And high above, an eagle was circling with its enormous wings outstretched, before diving down like a fighter plane to claim its prey far below. There was whistling, screeching, squawking and singing as birds of all shapes and sizes filled the branches of the trees that grew along the riverbank and back into the rain forest.

But birds were not the only life visible in the trees that overhung the river. There were monkeys! Little black-faced monkeys and larger gray ones, chattering and screaming as they leapt from tree to tree. Except for the ones that were fast asleep, of course, with their arms, legs and tails curled tightly around the branches.

And then to her right, EJ saw what looked like giant guinea pigs feeding on the river's edge. Capybaras. They were as big as sheep and there were masses of them munching the long grass along the muddy bank. Just ahead of them, a giant turtle was slowly making its way onto the bank.

For someone who loved animals as much as EJ, this was animal heaven. She could have just glided forever on her water scooter, watching the birds and animals make their way around the river.

But EJ wasn't the only thing gliding along the river, watching. All of a sudden, right in front of her, an otter scurried quickly out of the water and onto the bank. A flock of birds that had been calmly feeding suddenly began to squawk and flap excitedly and then flew swiftly up to the treetops. Everything seemed to be getting out of the water. And EJ got a funny feeling that maybe she should too. It was one of those funny feelings that actually wasn't funny at all—the feeling that someone, or something, was watching her...

Chapter •8

EJ didn't want to, but she *had* to turn around. She had to see what it was. Could it be a *SHADOW* agent? Already? She turned to see two enormous unblinking eyes moving smoothly through the water just behind her. EJ nearly jumped out of her skin! Attached to the enormous unblinking eyes was a large scaly body and long scaly tail that swung slowly from side to side, like a rudder in the water. As the eyes moved closer and closer toward EJ her heart now beat faster and faster.

Crocodile?

Moving slowly and carefully, EJ took her phone from her side pocket, snapped a photo, pressed "go," held her breath and waited. EJ had activated the animal app on her phone which could identify every animal in the world. In seconds, the photo appeared on the screen with text. There was good news and bad news. The good news was that it wasn't a crocodile: it was a cayman. According to her phone, a cayman was quite like a crocodile but smaller, and while it generally ate fish and small birds, it could also eat small mammals. That was the bad news. *I'm a small mammal,* thought EJ, starting to feel a little worried. Then there was a sentence that puzzled her. "SHINE recommends the use of charm."

Really? Are you serious? Was SHINE seriously suggesting that she start saying nice things to the cayman? Perhaps she should compliment it on its bright-yellow eyes or gush over its divine leathery scales? Just as she was beginning to think someone at the agency had gone crazy, EJ looked down and saw her bracelet with its silver charms glistening in the sunlight. *The little crocodile charm. Of course.*

Well, here goes nothing, thought EJ, as she twisted the tail of the crocodile charm, which produced a long, loud, high-pitched beep. The cayman stopped briefly and narrowed its eyes, but then continued toward EJ. It was getting very close to the back of her water scooter. EJ twisted again.

BEEEEEEEEEEP!

The noise was louder and higher this time. The cayman stared at EJ. She twisted the charm again.

BEEEEEEEEEEEEEEEEEEEEP!

This time the cayman blinked, stopped for a second and stared at EJ. She twisted the charm one more time.

BEEEEEEEEEEEEEEEEEEEEEEEEEEEEEP!

Suddenly the cayman turned sharply before diving down into the water. For a moment EJ was worried that it was about to appear right next to her, but when it resurfaced, it was far down the river, swimming in the opposite direction.

Lucky charm indeed, chuckled EJ. *I wonder if it works on older brothers?*

Thankfully, the rest of EJ's river trip was uneventful. After a while she moved off the big river toward a smaller one that became narrower and narrower. The beeps from the GPS on her phone were becoming louder and quicker. She was nearly there.

EJ turned toward the bank and pushed the ED button on her scooter. There was a loud cracking noise as the scooter boards came away from her boots. This was followed by what could only be described as a series of farting noises. EJ knew what that meant. The whole scooter was about to collapse and decompose. It was programmed for Eco-Deco, part of **SHINE's** eco-friendly equipment policy.

This was good because it meant agents didn't leave used equipment all over the place, but it was a rather smelly process.

Just as the farting noises became really loud, EJ jumped onto the riverbank, pulling the remains of the smelly scooter behind her. With one final squelch, it had gone. No one would ever know she had been here. Once the smell went away, at least.

EJ looked around and checked her GPS. According to the phone, she had arrived at 2 South 68 West. Now all she needed to do was to find the Butterfly Tree and the second message from *SHADOW*.

Standing on the riverbank, F112 was feeling a little jumpy. Not to mention squirmy and creepy. And she wasn't the only one. The floor of the rain forest seemed to be moving on its own—it was home to hundreds of every kind of insect you could imagine.

There were ants, mosquitos and grasshoppers (irritating, but at least EJ had her **SHINE** insect-repellent spray); there were snails and slugs (fine—

slimy but fine); there were little caterpillars and grubs (pretty gross) and there were spiders (completely gross and scary). EJ really didn't like spiders. They gave her the shivers. For a moment EJ wished she was back on the river, even with the cayman. EJ loved animals, and would do anything to help them, but she definitely preferred the kind you could cuddle. Spiders did not fit into that category however furry they got.

Yet for every hairy black spider, there was also something beautiful. There were red-and-black ladybugs, and little shiny beetles with hot-pink-and-turquoise shells, just as if someone had painted them in art class.

And there were butterflies—beautiful, vibrant, enormous butterflies with red-and-white spots, black-and-yellow stripes and deep, deep-blue wings. They were all flying and flitting around the plants on the rain forest floor. So where was the Butterfly Tree? What was the Butterfly Tree? Was it shaped like a butterfly?

EJ scanned the forest, looking for anything that might fit. Suddenly she felt something stroke her cheek. *Was that a spider?* EJ really hoped not. She jumped back in fright and as she spun around, she saw a swarm of blue butterflies ducking and weaving their way through the trees. *Worth following?* EJ had nothing else to go on.

EJ set off after the butterfly swarm, keeping her eyes on them as she ran through the rain forest— she couldn't lose them. Suddenly the swarm dived straight down and flew low to the ground as if they were trying to avoid something. Something fine and sticky. Something that EJ had just run into. *Yuck, a spider web! Please don't have a spider, please don't have a spider,* thought EJ, as she wiped her face and pulled the rest of the web out of her way. She was lucky, no spider in sight but also, no butterfly swarm. Where had it gone? Had she lost them? EJ started to run again, afraid the swarm had gotten too far ahead of her. She need not have worried. The butterfly swarm had stopped. Directly in front of EJ was a huge tree, dripping with sap, and crowded with thousands upon thousands of fluttering blue butterflies.

Chapter • 9

The Butterfly Tree! The butterflies were feeding off the sap, which is why there was so many of them. The tree reminded EJ of one of her favorite books that her mom used to read to her at bedtime. It was about an enchanted tree, the tallest tree in the forest, and one that was home to all sorts of fairy folk. It was a magical tree and if you climbed all the way up, there was a magic cloud and if you passed through it you could visit magical lands. There was also a little door at the foot of the tree...

Ouch! No little door here—just an enormous tree root and EJ had tripped over it. As she lay sprawled out at the base of the tree, she noticed some carvings on the bark in front of her. The carvings showed numbers—the second message! Who needed magic when you could just be clumsy!

EJ scrambled up and took a closer look. Sure enough, there were a series of numbers carved into the trunk.

38-40-36-2-18-14-16-40   42-32.

12-30-24-24-30-46

20-42-26-32   2-36-36-30-46-38.

4-36-18-8-14-10   40-30   38-18-40-10.

4-42-18-24-8-4-30-40

26-2-38-40-10-36

6-30-28-40-36-30-24.   10-28-40-10-36

12-30-36   6-30-8-10.

Yes, the second code! EJ pulled out a notepad from her backpack and carefully wrote the code down. It was another number code. She had expected that. She tried the same letter-number match as the first code, but that didn't work and EJ hadn't expected it to. *SHADOW* never used the same code twice, but the codes were always connected so it was probably still going to be a letter-number match, but which one?

EJ looked again, studying the code for patterns. Whenever she was stuck on a code, she would try lots of different ideas. It was the same with math problems. She knew they wouldn't always be the right ideas, but they helped her move toward the right one.

EJ enjoyed this part, trying to make sense of something that looked as if it was never going to make sense. She liked to have plenty of time to do it however, and on missions there was never plenty of time. EJ had to work quickly but carefully.

Is it the opposite of the last code? Does A=26 and Z=1? She looked again at the first bit of code—

38-40-36-2-18-14-16-40 42-32. She looked again.

That couldn't be right because some of the numbers were bigger than twenty-six. Hmmm.

Suddenly she realized that all the numbers were even numbers. Even numbers, two by two…

EJ had an idea. What if the second code went through the alphabet, two by two. Would that work? She flicked open her phone, opened up the codes app and scrolled down.

A	B	C	D	E	F	G	H
2	4	6	8	10	12	14	16
I	J	K	L	M	N	O	P
18	20	22	24	26	28	30	32
Q	R	S	T	U	V	W	X
34	36	38	40	42	44	46	48
Y	Z						
50	52						

EJ tried the first word. I've still got it, she smiled to herself, and in next to no time she had cracked the rest of the code.

For EJ12's Eyes Only

(Message intercepted from SHADOW)

38-40-36-2-18-14-16-40   42-32.
S T R A I G H T U P.
12-30-24-24-30-46
F O L L O W
20-42-26-32 2-36-36-30-46-38.
J U M P A R R O W S.
4-36-18-8-14-10 40-30 38-18-40-10.
B R I D G E T O S I T E.
4-42-18-24-8-4-30-40
B U I L D B O T
26-2-38-40-10-36
M A S T E R
6-30-28-40-36-30-24. 10-28-40-10-36
C O N T R O L. E N T E R
12-30-36 6-30-8-10
F O R C O D E.

What could it possibly mean? She would need some help with this one. EJ remembered her instructions. She had to call **SHINE** as soon as she found the second message. She pressed the top secret HQ app on her phone, texted the message from *SHADOW* and waited.

After a few seconds, her phone rang.

"EJ12," she answered.

"A1," came the voice at the other end. "Well done, EJ12."

"Thanks, A1, but even though I cracked the code, I don't understand the message."

"Keep working on it, EJ12," urged A1. "I can help you with one thing though. We know *SHADOW* has been working on a surveillance system that can be run completely automatically from a master control. If I am not mistaken, the problem they are having with Project Green Eye may well be a bug in the system of that master control."

"Well, there are certainly enough bugs here," said EJ looking around.

"Very funny, EJ. But not so funny is that *SHADOW* knows we are on to Project Green Eye so you need to figure it out quickly—very quickly. We have the jump on *SHADOW*, but they have leapt into action. You probably only have a couple of hours before they arrive in the rain forest to stop us from stopping them. I'll contact you if there are any more updates, but for now, get going, EJ12."

Get going, but where?

EJ12 needed to figure out that message, and fast. She flicked to the alarm app on her phone and set it for two hours, with a reminder every thirty minutes. She was now in a race against *SHADOW* and needed to keep track of the time. Then she looked at the message again. *SHADOW* never seemed to give straightforward instructions. *What were jump arrows?* she thought. *And hello—a buildbot?*

One step at a time, thought EJ. *Don't get ahead of yourself. Straight up? Okay, I can do that,* thought EJ. She looked straight up but was immediately blinded by the sun. EJ squinted, but still the bright rays piercing through the leaves made it impossible to see. She reached into her backpack and pulled out her sunglasses. A1 was right—sometimes common sense was just what a secret agent needed. *Much better*, thought EJ, as she put them on, *and rather stylish as well!*

Now she could see a thick leafy vine that seemed to grow right up to the top of the tree. EJ guessed she would need to climb "straight up" that vine, but what was she going to do about all those butterflies? She needed to grip the vine with her hands and climb up the tree with her feet—but that meant stepping on an awful lot of butterflies. *No way.* She needed another plan. She tried to shoo the butterflies away, but there were simply too many. As fast as some flew off, others flew back again, all very keen to continue feeding on the tree sap. It was hopeless. EJ really needed to get up that tree, and time was ticking away.

She sat on the ground and thought hard. Whenever she got stuck on something, she liked to sit quietly and see if she could puzzle it out. She liked to sort things in her mind in an orderly way.

She hated timed tests, but now that she was in one, she needed to think calmly and quickly—easier said than done. As she thought, she started to fiddle with her charm bracelet. Then she remembered. *The butterfly charm!* How slow could a secret agent be?

"Here goes," said EJ and she twisted the butterfly charm. A small puff of crimson smoke floated up into the air. It had a sickly sweet smell. Instantly, the butterflies came darting toward it. *This must be the butterfly version of chocolate*, thought EJ. She kept twisting the charm as she moved away from the tree. The butterflies followed the crimson smoke and sweet smell, and soon the whole swarm had moved away from the Butterfly Tree, which was now more like an Ex-Butterfly Tree. Now the trunk was clearly visible and EJ could see a green arrow pointing straight up etched into the bark. She was on the right track, or should that be tree?

Chapter •10

EJ grabbed the vine with both hands and began to climb. At gymnastics, her team was always practicing on the ropes. They first climbed straight up with both their arms and legs. Then, and it hurt even to remember, they let their legs hang loose and climbed straight up, pulling themselves with their arms only. *This vine should be easy compared to that.* EJ gripped the trunk with her boots and started climbing.

The first thirty feet were easy, the next thirty feet were easy-ish, and the next thirty feet were not easy at all! Ninety feet up with at least another thirty to go, EJ was beginning to wish she'd saved a little more energy at the start. Her arms and legs ached and she was struggling just to hold on. But she needed to get to the top. She took a deep breath and hauled herself up with her arms. One pull at a time, EJ continued slowly upward.

Finally, with one last heave, she reached the top of the vine. She had also climbed all the way up through the trees and was now on top of the rain forest canopy. If she had not already been out of breath, the view would have taken her breath away. EJ was sitting atop the most beautiful rain forest she had ever seen.

Tall, tall trees shot straight up into the air and then exploded with a burst of leaves at the top. Deep-green vines and brightly colored flowers twisted around their branches, almost strangling the trees in shocks of color. The flowers were enormous and the strangest, most unusual shapes and colors EJ had ever seen. Indeed, if she wasn't seeing it with her own eyes, she would have said they were made up—like flowers in a cartoon. There were masses of orange and purple flowers that looked like huge balls of cotton candy stuck on the end of bright-green sticks, all lined up in a row. There were pink-and-blue flowers with petals that looked like little drooping umbrellas. There were bright-red flowers that shot through the light-green vines like beautiful but dangerous sword-like thorns.

Now she could also see all the birds she had watched from the river close up. In fact, EJ had a bird's-eye view of the birds. Parrots and toucans dashed between the trees, squawking and screeching. There were crazy-looking woodpeckers hammering into the tree trunks while tiny birds hopped from leaf to leaf.

Beep-Beep Beep-Beep

The first alarm. *No time to admire the view, I have to keep moving. Where to now?* EJ looked around and noticed a second arrow, this time pointing left toward another thick green vine. She took her binoculars out of her backpack and looked carefully around her, scanning the trees. Then she saw it, another tree a short distance away, with another arrow and then another vine. And beyond that, there was yet another tree with an arrow and yet another vine. *I get it*, thought EJ. *Jump arrows!* EJ realized she had to jump from one tree to the next by swinging from the vines. *This is going to be interesting*, she thought. *Why would anyone want to swing from vine to vine?* She decided **SHADOW** must have monkeys for agents!

There was nothing for it. EJ had to jump. The arrows would take her closer to Project Green Eye and the only way to travel through the dense rain forest was to jump from tree to tree.

EJ felt her muscles tighten and her mouth dry out, just like when she was on the beam at the gym. But hold on, that was Emma Jacks, wimpy gymnast —not EJ12, secret agent, code-cracker extraordinaire and current leader of the **SHINE** Shining Stars competition. And besides, it was jumping up that was the problem and this was jumping across. Okay, it was jumping from tree to tree. And it wasn't quite the same as in the gym. But it was still jumping across. Even Emma Jacks could do that!

It was just like the old movies she and her mom loved to watch together—the ones where the hero would swing her way across the jungle to save the boy who was being held prisoner by a secret jungle tribe. EJ knew exactly what she needed to do. *Reach out for the vine, pull it back, then swing over and jump to the next tree.* Timing would be important, and so was time, which was beginning to run out. EJ needed to jump straight in.

She pulled back the first vine, leapt out of the tree and swung.

Whoosh!

Wow! It was as if she were flying through the rain forest! EJ had never had so much fun! In fact, she was having so much fun that she missed her jump and swung all the way back to the first tree.

Okay, second time lucky and concentrate, she thought. She pulled back and swung again.

whoosh!

This time, just as she reached the highest point in the arc of the swing, she lined up the next tree. *Here it comes, here it comes. Ready, set, jump!*

EJ landed right on a branch, exactly where she needed to be, next to the second jump arrow. She had made it—and she couldn't wait to do it again! She looked for the next vine and grabbed it.

whoosh!

She was off again. This time it was a longer vine and therefore a longer, slower swing. But EJ timed her jump perfectly and landed in the next tree, right beside another green jump arrow. She jumped and swung, swung and jumped all the way through the rain forest. *If only Lauren could see me now! If only Nema could see me now! This would stop her mean comments.* Part of her was hoping she could go on swinging and jumping forever, but eventually she landed on a branch next to an arrow that pointed straight down.

Down? This time there was no vine to swing on and no branches below her to help her climb down to the forest floor. And then suddenly, EJ heard a crack. She turned quickly, but there was nothing to see. Despite this, EJ knew that something, or someone, was close by.

Chapter • 11

For the second time that day, EJ had the feeling that someone was watching her. She hated that feeling. She turned her head slowly from side to side, scanning the treetops around her. After a while, she saw them: two shiny black eyes, blinking quietly in the dappled sunlight. These eyes didn't look threatening though, they looked curious, even friendly. But what did they belong to?

Suddenly EJ had an idea. She grabbed a round-looking fruit that was hanging from an overhead branch. Slowly and quietly, she broke it open and put a small piece in the palm of her hand. Then she stretched out her arm, stayed perfectly still and waited.

Nothing happened, but EJ could see the little eyes still looking at her. *Hmmm*, she thought and then said out loud, "Oh well, I guess I'll eat it then." She put some fruit in her mouth and chewed. Not bad, and maybe her little trick would work. She took another piece of fruit and put that in her hand and held it out again. Just as she began to move it toward her mouth again a little furry arm appeared and snatched the fruit from her hand. EJ presented another piece. "That was nice, wasn't it?" she whispered softly. "Come down here where I can see you!"

Four pieces of fruit later, a tiny monkey jumped lightly onto EJ's lap and looked straight up at her. She was so cute—small with a tiny little black head and a white face. She looked as if she was wearing a mask, like a little bank robber! A little baby monkey bank robber. But what sort of monkey?

As the monkey nibbled on the fruit, EJ eased her phone out of her pocket and snapped a photo. Within seconds, the screen displayed text about her new little friend. She was a squirrel monkey.

SQUIRREL MONKEYS ARE THE BEST JUMPERS OF ALL THE MONKEYS AND MAKE THEIR WAY THROUGH THE RAIN FOREST BY JUMPING FROM TREE TO TREE. THEY EAT SPIDERS, INSECTS, EGGS, FRUIT AND NUTS. THEY USUALLY LIVE IN GROUPS OF UP TO THIRTY BUT ARE FACING EXTINCTION DUE TO LOSS OF THEIR NATURAL HABITAT.

"So where are all your friends?" EJ wondered aloud. The little squirrel monkey seemed to be alone, but she was still only a baby. EJ saw some nuts and offered them. The monkey seemed to like them even more than the fruit, so EJ put some extras in her pocket. Then, the squirrel monkey suddenly leapt off EJ's lap and jumped down. EJ peered down below after her. She saw that the monkey had landed on what looked like a bed of ferns, growing out of the side of the tree trunk a few feet below. "Hey!" she called. "Are you telling me that's the only way down?"

EJ was heavier than the monkey, but the ferns looked very soft. She grabbed hold of the overhead branch, dropped her legs down and put one foot on the ferns. *So far, so good.* She put her other foot on the ferns, then let go of the branch. *Bad move.*

Crash!

EJ fell straight through the bed of ferns and bounced from leafy branch to ferns to leafy branch down the length of the tree.

Splat!

Splat!

DOUBLE Splat!

Just when she thought it was getting slightly ridiculous, EJ realized she had finally reached the ground. And there was her little monkey friend, sitting on top of the bush that EJ had just landed in. The little monkey had found herself a nut and was chewing away happily.

"Thanks a lot for that—I think!" said EJ, as she picked herself up and brushed herself off. The monkey almost looked as if she was waiting for EJ—at least until she turned tail and scurried off into the rain forest.

"Hey, wait for me!" shouted EJ. She pushed her way out of the bushes and chased the monkey through the undergrowth until they both arrived at a clearing. Except it wasn't a natural clearing: it was more like a track, a man-made track that had been carelessly hacked through the rain forest.

This man-made track has destroyed some of the rain forest trees, thought EJ. *It's ugly and wrong!*

It had to be something to do with *SHADOW*. And sure enough, nailed to one of the sawn-off tree trunks was another green arrow.

"You know, you're a pretty useful mission buddy," said EJ to the little squirrel monkey. "And if you're coming with me, then you better have a name and given you love them so much, how about Nuts?"

Nuts tilted her head first one way and then the other and let out a loud shriek.

"I'll take that as a 'yes,'" smiled EJ. "Hey! Where are you going now?"

Nuts had taken off again, running and jumping down the track, and EJ had to run as fast as she could to keep up. Suddenly the little monkey stopped dead in her tracks. Actually, the whole track stopped and the whole forest stopped too—or rather, it dropped. The rain forest floor dropped away sharply to a canyon, hundreds of feet deep.

Luckily for EJ, there was a bridge across the canyon to get to the other side. Unluckily for EJ, it was a rope bridge—with lots of holes. EJ took out her binoculars and turned them to the land across the other side of the canyon. She could hardly believe what she was seeing. There was no rain forest and no giant towering trees. There were no more enormous colorful flowers, twisting vines, leafy canopy or squawking parrots and toucans. Where the rain forest should have been, there was just brown dirt and blackened trunks of burned and sawn-off trees. The forest had been cleared and in the middle of the bare ground stood exactly what EJ had been looking for. A huge satellite dish with the letters S-H-A-D-O-W written on the side! EJ had found Project Green Eye.

Chapter •12

Beep-Beep Beep-Beep

EJ's alarm was going off again and now there was just one hour left, at the most, before a *SHADOW* agent—or agents—would arrive to save what EJ12 now had to destroy.

EJ grabbed her phone. It was time to report back to **SHINE HQ**.

"EJ12, go ahead," said A1.

"I've located Project Green Eye," EJ started.

"That's excellent, well done."

"But I'm not there yet. There's a deep canyon between me and the site," EJ continued.

"That's bad."

"There's an old rope bridge across the canyon, with a kind of platform in the middle on top of an old wooden tower," EJ explained.

"That's good."

"But the rope bridge is full of holes and the tower looks as if it might collapse any second. That's bad," EJ finished.

"No, that's good!" said A1 on the other end of the line. "You're a gymnast, EJ12. And gymnasts know how to jump!"

This one doesn't, thought EJ miserably. But she wasn't going to tell A1 that. Then she heard a buzzing noise coming from SHINE HQ.

"EJ12," said A1 urgently. "That was the *SHADOW* alert light again. It's what we feared. *SHADOW* knows that we intercepted the second message and has set the third and final message to self-destruct. That may take some time, but according to our calculations, you probably have less than an hour to find the third message and crack the code. Good luck, EJ12. **SHINE** out."

EJ picked up her binoculars and looked across to the Project Green Eye site. She was so close and yet so far. The rope bridge reminded EJ of a challenge she had done at camp last year. You had to cross a small creek on a set of two ropes, holding on to the top rope with your arms and moving along the bottom rope with your feet. But that rope bridge had only been about three feet above the water—this one was quite a bit higher and above a canyon. *Well*, thought EJ to herself, *it's a bit different from camp, but really the same challenge. I need to concentrate and I need to have balance.*

Nuts certainly had balance. The little monkey took one big leap, landed on the bridge and ran along it nimbly, without a care. After a few feet, the monkey stopped and looked back at EJ.

"Smarty monkey!" she shouted, her voice echoing across the canyon below. *A1 was right—I'm a gymnast*, thought EJ, as she climbed nervously onto the rope bridge. *I have balance too!*

The bridge was made up of three main ropes. There were two ropes at the top, and EJ grasped one tightly with each hand. There was a single rope at the base, which was joined to the top ropes by smaller loops—many of which were broken or missing. EJ balanced her boots on the bottom rope and slowly began to edge her way across.

If this was a movie, EJ thought, *people would say, "Don't look down! Whatever you do, don't look down!"* And now, as EJ looked down, she understood why. It was a long, long, long way down! In fact, the more she looked down, the more she thought about falling instead of moving. EJ paused. What did that remind her of? Her mind went blank. *Oh well, no time to think about it now.* She had a super-wobbly bridge to cross.

"Just look up!" EJ told herself and she took a deep breath. Then she forced herself to look straight ahead and told her body, not her mind, to do the walking. It was working well, until halfway across EJ's right foot slipped on the base rope and she fell through one of the loops as she tried to regain her balance. Clinging on to the top ropes and staring down into the valley far below, EJ gulped. She would have to be more careful. She swung her feet around to find the base rope, hauled herself upright, put one foot forward and started again. At last she made it to the platform in the middle. Halfway there, but she was running out of time.

From her perch on the platform, high above the canyon floor, EJ could see the Project Green Eye site more clearly. And she could hear it now too. There was a whirring noise, lots of whirring noises actually, but where were they coming from? EJ pulled out her binoculars and took a closer look.

Moving around and around the satellite dish was a small army of little machines on wheels. The machines seemed to have arms, arms holding building tools. *Robots with building tools? Builder robots? Buildbots!*

How could she not have figured out that one? EJ did sometimes wonder how she had gotten into the code-cracking division! However, these buildbots weren't building—they weren't doing anything except going around and around in circles. EJ knew from her **SHINE** training on spy satellite systems that it was the satellite dish, not the things building it, that was supposed to go around in circles. So that had to be the problem *SHADOW* had written about in the first message. Somehow, the buildbots had lost it! A1 had been right, there must be a problem with the Master Control that ran the buildbots.

And then, as she scanned across the building site, EJ noticed something else. Just past the satellite dish, EJ could see rows and rows of large wooden crates. She adjusted the binoculars so she could make out the label on one of them.

SHIP DIRECT TO SHADOW

Ship what? What has SHADOW packed in the crates? thought E J. She readjusted the binoculars and scanned the crates again. This time she saw another label.

THIS WAY UP
—
LIVE
ANIMALS

Live animals? Being shipped to SHADOW? Away from their home in the rain forest? It looked as if SHADOW was stealing wild animals from a World Heritage protected area. *But for what? Private zoos? Collectors? Or something worse?* E J couldn't bear to think about it. It was bad enough that SHADOW had destroyed part of the animals' home, but to round them all up and steal them was outrageous. *Would SHADOW stop at nothing?* E J wondered. *Do they really think they can get away with it?*

"I don't think so," EJ said to herself. "No way, not with EJ!" And despite being in a tense situation, she smiled, feeling rather happy with that little saying. There was no way these animals were going anywhere other than back into the rain forest.

EJ stuffed her binoculars into her backpack. Now more than ever, she needed to get across the last stretch of bridge. And she had to do it quickly.

Chapter • 13

Now that she was closer, EJ discovered three things about the last stretch of the bridge. First, it wasn't really a whole rope bridge anymore. No doubt it used to be a whole rope bridge, but now it was more like a series of holes with a bit of rope joining them together. Big holes. The sort of holes you always saw people falling through in the movies.

Second, for the last few feet before the bridge reached the cliffs on the other side of the canyon, there were only the two top ropes left. No bottom rope.

And the third thing EJ noticed made everything else a lot worse. A strong wind was starting to blow. All the birds were hang gliding in the stiff breeze rather than flying, and the bridge was starting to swing from side to side.

Now EJ felt sick—really sick. She swallowed deeply, but her mouth had gone completely dry. She felt her legs tighten and then go wobbly, like jelly. She knew exactly what needed to be done and that was exactly what was making her feel sick. All of a sudden, she felt more like Emma Jacks than EJ12. She would have to jump across the end of the bridge with big jumps, really big jumps, and she was not totally sure that she could.

And then, just to make matters worse, it started to rain. Not little spots of rain or a light shower, but big, wet rain. Rain forest rain. *Excellent*, thought EJ. *The whole mission now depends on me being able to do enormously big jumps in the howling wind and pouring rain.*

EJ needed something extra to help her do this. It was definitely time to use the BEST system.

EJ flicked her phone to video mode and called Hannah.

"Hey, Em, where are you? Okay, I know you can't answer that. What's up?" asked Hannah cheerily.

"I'm here," said EJ, swinging her phone around so her friend could see her. "And I came from there," she continued, swinging the phone around to show the first bridge. "And now I need to get over there," she finished, swinging the phone back to the last stretch of the bridge and zooming in, "on that!"

"Oh," said Hannah. "That's not much of a bridge, is it?"

"No. You can see my problem."

"I can," Hannah replied. "But how long is that gap at the end?"

"Three feet or so, maybe a little bit more."

"Well, that's all right, then!" Hannah chuckled.

"What do you mean?"

"That's no more than the high jump in your gymnastics routine," Hannah explained.

"You mean the one I can't do."

"No, the one you can do, but you psyche yourself

out of doing by thinking about the fall, not the jump. You can do this easily. Just concentrate on the jump, a big, long, beautiful jump, as if you have wings."

"I'm not sure that will work…"

"Hey, Em," said Hannah. "What's the best that can happen?"

"I can't tell you that, Han," said EJ, and she thought how close she was to completing her mission, shutting down Project Green Eye and rescuing all those animals. "But it's good, really good. Actually it's completely awesome. Maybe I can do the jump, but I just think—"

"So stop thinking and fly. What are you waiting for—don't be nuts!"

That reminded her. *Where's Nuts?* EJ looked up. She'd been following Nuts the whole way across the bridge. She watched as the little squirrel monkey took a flying leap from the end of the bridge, scrabbled up the cliff face, turned and sat there on the other side of the canyon, waiting.

Beep-Beep Beep-Beep

Half an hour to go. What am I waiting for?

And then suddenly, standing on a wobbly rope bridge in the wind and rain, everything became clear to EJ12. She had jumped out of planes and onto riverbanks. She had leapt from trees to vines and vines to trees. She had edged her way across the first stretch of the bridge. She was going to do this jump too. EJ suddenly got it, Hannah believed she could do the jump and now so did she. She really did, she could feel it. EJ's mouth was no longer dry and she suddenly felt lighter. She smiled to herself. She was ready.

"Watch out, Nuts. I'm coming after you!" she yelled.

EJ climbed onto the bridge and walked along a little. When she came to a gap in the base rope she slid her hands along the top ropes and jumped. She did this again and again until she was nearly across. Just one more jump, and it needed to be the biggest jump of all. EJ began to think… *Actually, perhaps I am not ready, perhaps I should think…*

But her friend, still on the end of the phone, knew her well.

"Don't start thinking, Em. Just do it!"

Something clicked in EJ's brain. She could do this jump—she could feel it. She thought of all the animals waiting for rescue on the other side. Then she closed her eyes and imagined the perfect flying jump. She could do it! She could see it! She knew it!

EJ took two steps, as long as the holes in the base rope allowed, and then she jumped up across the last big gap. It was biggest, highest, longest leap of her life. She flew off the bridge and, with legs fully outstretched, jumped onto the top of the cliff. She stuck the landing on both feet and then, just because she felt like it, she did a perfect backflip.

"Show-off!" shouted Hannah gleefully.

EJ stood on the cliff and looked back. Had she really done that?

"That was awesome! Because you were holding the phone, I felt like I did the jump with you," said Hannah. "Good luck and see you back at school."

"Thanks, Han, I couldn't have done it without you," said EJ.

"Actually, you could have," replied her friend, laughing, "but I am glad I could help. Now go save something!"

EJ grinned. She was officially awesome! She rocked! She jumped!

But there was no time for celebrating. There was now less than thirty minutes until the third and final *SHADOW* message would self-destruct. She needed to find that message and decode it quickly.

Piinngg!

It was a text from HQ

ATTENTION EJ12

SHADOW AIRCRAFT HAVE BEEN DETECTED IN AREA. BE QUICK—AND BE CAREFUL.

Make that super-quick, thought EJ. She reviewed her situation. There was a lot to do. There were buildbots to manage, a satellite dish to destroy, and animals to return to the rain forest. But EJ12 was on a roll and nothing was going to stop her now.

Chapter •14

EJ looked around the satellite site and wondered. *Buildbot Master Control? Quick,* thought EJ. *Where is it?* Her spy training clicked in as she scanned from left to right, taking in everything, and then back again right to left. She saw the crates, the satellite dish and Nuts, who was sitting on a small pole. A small pole with a sign at the top.

**BUILDBOT
MASTER CONTROL**

"Okay, another spy point to you, Nuts," said EJ. "That was too easy." She rewarded her little furry friend with another nut. As Nuts chewed away, EJ found a small cabinet at the bottom of the pole. Locked. She pulled up her charm bracelet and tried the lock with the key.

"I love **SHINE**," laughed EJ. The key turned the lock without a problem. The door opened revealing a tiny panel of buttons—Buildbot Master Control. EJ pushed a few random buttons, but nothing happened. Then a message flashed up on the screen.

```
ENTER
SECURITY CODE
```

What code? The second message had said "enter for code." *But what did that mean? Think, EJ, think.* EJ scanned the panel, her mind racing. It was like a tiny keyboard—were some of the letters or numbers the code? Her eyes moved from left to right, working her way across the panel, past the enter key. *The enter key! Could it really be that simple? Only one way to find out,* thought EJ. She hit the enter button and hoped she was right.

Another message flashed up on the screen.

63-42-36-45-9-33

EJ always feared the final code as it was usually the most difficult, so she was a bit surprised to see that it was so short.

Hmmm, a short code but not an easy code. There are some pretty big numbers there, except for the 9. And some are odd and some are even.

EJ kept looking at the numbers, willing a pattern to appear. She knew those numbers would have to have something in common, but what?

Is it 9? EJ wondered. *Let's see.*

4 x 9 is 36 and 5 x 9 is 45 and 7 x 9 is 63.

So far so good. But hold on, 9 doesn't go into 42 or 33.

EJ had reached a dead end. Or had she?

But hang on, they can all be divided into 3, can't they?

The first code went in 1s, the second in 2s. Was the third code in 3s?

EJ flicked to her calculator app and punched in the numbers.

21 x 3 is 63

14 x 3 is 42

12 x 3 is 36

15 x 3 is 45

3 x 3 is 9

Yes! EJ knew she had it now

11 x 3 is 33!

That has to be it. EJ opened up her code app and flicked through to find the code table. *There it is.*

A	B	C	D	E	F	G	H
3	6	9	12	15	18	21	24
I	J	K	L	M	N	O	P
27	30	33	36	39	42	45	48
Q	R	S	T	U	V	W	X
51	54	57	60	63	66	69	72
Y	Z						
75	78						

U N L O C K

63-42-36-45-9-33

"Arrggh," groaned EJ. "I should have guessed that one without even cracking the code!"

But she wasn't about to complain. All three codes had now been cracked. She had gotten to them before

SHADOW and it looked like her perfect mission record was still intact.

She keyed it in and waited. A little green flashing light on the control panel told EJ what *SHADOW* already knew. There was a buildbot malfunction. She pressed enter again and another message appeared on the screen.

FIX OR
REPROGRAM?

EJ thought for a minute and smiled. Reprogram, what a great idea! She typed furiously into the control panel. Everything was going to be okay.

Within seconds, the buildbots stopped moving in crazy circles. But instead of going back to building the satellite dish, they began to take it apart. Quickly. Pretty soon, Project Green Eye was just a heap of scrap metal on the ground.

"Love your work, bots!" said EJ, pressing another few buttons. This time the buildbots headed toward the packing crates.

EJ grinned. Her plan was working perfectly. The buildbots positioned themselves next to the crates and then stopped. There was a series of beeps and with one swift movement, each buildbot unbolted a crate and pulled the door open.

Suddenly there were animals everywhere! Baby spider monkeys, parrots, jaguars, vampire bats, squirrel monkeys and howler monkeys—all crying out for their mothers.

EJ hit the pause button and shut the buildbots down. As soon as the clanking and beeping from the robots stopped, the most amazing thing happened. Out of the rain forest beyond the huge bare clearing, a vast mass of animals came squeaking, squawking, growling, hissing and whistling into view. The parents were coming to get their babies and take them back into the safety of the forest.

Soon there was only one baby animal left. Nuts.

111

"Where's *your* mom?" said EJ.

Nuts whistled and leapt onto EJ's head. Maybe Nuts really was all alone.

Once the site was cleared of the animals, EJ re-hit the pause button and the buildbots started up again. But this time they put themselves into the packing crates and closed the doors behind them.

"No more building for you, bots!" EJ shouted. She keyed in one more set of instructions, grabbed Nuts and ran for cover. They hit the ground a short distance away and she covered Nuts' ears.

KABOOM!

The buildbots had self-destructed inside the wooden crates and the explosion had destroyed what was left of the satellite dish. Nothing remained of Project Green Eye.

Chapter •15

EJ sat up, feeling rather pleased with herself. Nuts slid her hand into EJ's pocket. She felt rather pleased about getting another nut. EJ took out her phone. It was time to go home. She pressed 4-6-6-3 into the keypad and a woman's voice answered immediately.

"**SHINE** Home Delivery Service—straight to your door anytime, anywhere."

"Agent EJ12 requesting home delivery," replied EJ. Looking at Nuts, she added, "For two."

"No problem, EJ12. We have locked in your coordinates with transportation on standby in the area. It won't be long."

She wasn't kidding. A few minutes later, EJ heard the chop-chop-chop of helicopter blades.

"Hold on tight, Nuts," said EJ. "It's going to get pretty blowy. In fact, you better stay in here." She put the little monkey inside her backpack.

The helicopter hovered over the clearing and lowered a rope ladder.

A familiar voice boomed out over the noise of the blades. "EJ12, this is LP30. Jump on the ladder and we'll winch you up."

More rope, thought EJ. *At least this one leads somewhere. Up we go!*

As EJ climbed, the chopper winched and she was soon inside the cockpit with LP30.

"Welcome back, EJ12. Great job! And just in time too—look out the side window and check what's coming toward us."

EJ turned to see another helicopter far off in the distance, but coming closer all the time. A few seconds later, she could make out the letters on the side with her binoculars—S, H, A...

"*SHADOW?*" said EJ, holding her breath.

"You bet," replied LP30.

"But they're too late," smiled EJ. "I found the last message before they could destroy it, so Project Green Eye is no more! Do you think they'll follow us?"

"Let's not hang around to find out," said LP30. "And besides, I have something to show you."

The chopper turned sharply down toward the river and followed the path of the water.

"I hope they're still there," said LP30. "Let's go lower and see."

They were skimming along the surface of the river. EJ thought that if she dangled her feet outside the helicopter, she could probably feel the water rushing through her toes. And then she saw them —dolphins. *Pink* dolphins! A whole school of them leaping and diving along the river as if they were escorting EJ home.

"Wow!" exclaimed EJ.

"Aren't they beautiful?" cried LP30 over the noise of chopper. "They're botos—river dolphins—and they only live in this part of the world."

"They're amazing," EJ shouted. "And so pink!"

They finally left the river and headed home. EJ settled into the seat, took Nuts out of her backpack and smiled as the little monkey nestled into her lap.

"EJ12, it's A1 on the air video phone," said LP30. "Time to report in."

"Hello, A1," said EJ, feeling relaxed. "Mission complete. Project Green Eye dismantled. Buildbots destroyed. And all baby animals safely returned to the rain forest. Well, all except one…"

"EJ12?"

"I seem to have found a friend," EJ explained, as she held Nuts up to the screen. "She's lost her mother and looks much too young to fend for herself."

"You made the right decision, EJ12. We'll send her to a native animal sanctuary where you can be sure she will be well cared for. You will also be pleased to know that **SHINE** is preparing to replant the cleared area in the rain forest. The trees will grow quickly and soon no one will ever know that *SHADOW* was there."

"That's fantastic," said EJ.

"Yes but not only that," continued A1, "it will take *SHADOW* a long time to make a new batch of buildbots as well as find another satellite base location. Good work, EJ12. We've really got the jump on them now!"

Enough of the jumping thing, thought EJ12. *I've got the message.*

"Oh and EJ, good luck in the gymnastics meet this weekend," said A1. "You will be great, I know you will. That's all, EJ12. **SHINE** out." The phone disconnected.

The gymnastics meet. EJ had forgotten about that, but now that she was thinking about it again, she realized she no longer felt nervous. With all the leaping around she'd done lately, she finally realized what everyone else—Lauren, Hannah, A1—had seemed to know already. She could jump high, as high as anyone else, maybe even higher—she just had to believe in herself.

I can do it, thought EJ. *I did do it. Can I do it again? Yes I can, I know I can.*

EJ was proud of herself yet also tired. As she was settling down for an in-flight snooze, she noticed the little heart with wings on her charm bracelet.

Hey, I didn't use that one, she thought. *I wonder what it does.*

EJ twisted the little charm and as she did, a small inscription appeared.

Jump and you will find your wings.

EJ thought back over the mission and as she read the inscription again, she smiled to herself as she realized that she had done just that. She had jumped. She had trusted herself and she had found her wings.

With the smile still on her face, EJ fell asleep.

Chapter • 16

The following Saturday was the big day. The gymnastics meet, but not just any meet: *the* meet, the State Finals. Emma and the girls on her team had practiced all year for this day and now here it was.

The gym arena was packed to capacity with gymnasts, their coaches and the family and friends who had come to support them. And on a table, on the far side of the arena, stood the trophies and medals, shining, waiting to be awarded.

The girls on Emma's gymnastics team were going through their warm-up with Lauren. They were wearing their team leotards and they looked fabulous. They were a lilac color with beautiful, glittery starbursts shooting across the front and down the top of the long sleeves. Finally, for the finishing touch, all the girls on the team had done their hair the same way—high ponytails with lilac elastics and deep-lilac ribbons.

"Our leos are the best, don't you think, Em?" said Hannah. "If they were judging on leotards, we would medal for sure."

Emma smiled at her friend and they gave each other an excited hug. They were ready.

First up was floor exercise, then vault and bars. Emma, Hannah, Nema and Isi, the fourth member of the team, all moved through their routines strongly. Each of them did the best routine they had done all year and Lauren was confident that the girls would score well. They were in with a real chance for a medal. With only one rotation to go, you could feel the excitement in the arena.

It was time for Emma's team to do their beam routines. Nema went first and did well with only a few wobbles as she did her handstand. Even though she had done a good job, Emma could tell Nema was disappointed.

"Good job, Nema," said Emma. "Don't worry about the handstand, your dismount was great."

"*You* might not worry about the handstand, but I do," sniffed Nema.

"Don't worry about her, Em," whispered Hannah. "She's just angry at herself. Look, Isi is about to start her routine." Hannah turned back toward the beam and cried, "Go, Is!"

Isi did the best routine she had done all season and all the girls cheered. Then it was Hannah's turn. Hannah almost flew onto the beam and skipped through the routine, smiling all the way. This time she didn't fall off and straight after a perfect dismount, she bounced over to her team and high-fived everyone, even a reluctant Nema.

So far the team had done well, really well. And now it was Emma's turn.

Emma sprang onto the beam and swung into action. She completed the first half of the routine smoothly and strongly. She walked to the end of the beam and spun around, moving into position for the split jumps. The big jumps, the highlight of the routine.

Emma stopped for a moment, raised her arms and smiled. Then, almost without thinking, and with an enormous smile still on her face, she looked straight ahead, stretched her legs and leapt into the highest, strongest split jump of the day. She followed up with another jump, just as high. She then almost glided into her handstand, which she held perfectly, before returning to stand at the end of the beam. She then ran to the other end of the beam and flipped off, onto the landing mat. Emma stuck the landing firmly on two feet. Just as she knew she would.

The audience broke into applause.

"I did it," said Emma to herself.

"Way to go!" cried Hannah giving Emma a big hug. Then she lowered her voice to a whisper, "Show-off—again!"

For once Nema was at a loss for words, which was an unexpected bonus. She just stood by the beam, her mouth wide-open in disbelief.

Lauren, normally a very calm person, leapt to her feet and cheered. "Emma Jacks, that was awesome!" she cried. "It was almost as if you had wings, you jumped so high. We will medal for sure now. Where did that all come from?"

"From me," said Emma, beaming, and then added to herself, *with a little help from EJ12.*

Emma Jacks and EJ12 return in

BOOK 3
IN THE DARK

Did you miss Book 1?

EJ12

GIRL HERO

HOT & COLD

The heat is on as someone seems to be melting the polar ice cap.

Special Agent EJ12 needs to crack the codes and keep her cool to put the evildoer's plan back on ice.
That's the easy part.

As EJ12, Emma Jacks can do anything.

So why can't she handle the school Ice Queen of Mean, Nema?

Perhaps she can after all...

Read Book 3 next!

EJ12 GIRL HERO
IN THE DARK

SHINE's solar energy station is under threat from the evil agency SHADOW.

Special Agent EJ12 needs to lighten up. She must crack SHADOW's codes and overcome her fears to stop them before they turn the lights out on the SHINE network. That's the easy part.

As EJ12, Emma Jacks can do anything.

So why is she worried about going to her best friend's slumber party?

Perhaps she isn't after all...

And don't miss Book 4!

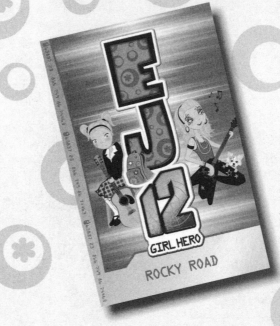

Evil Agency SHADOW is really rocking the SHINE network. SHINE knows they are planning something, but how are they sending their messages?

Special Agent EJ12 must not miss a beat. This time she needs to find the code as well as pull the curtain down on SHADOW.
That's the easy part.

As EJ12, Emma Jacks can do anything.

So why can't she perform with her friends at the school concert?

Perhaps she can after all...